Perfect Snow

Barbara Reid

Albert Whitman & Company
Chicago, Illinois

For Zoe who built it,
Tara who remembered,
and Julie, Marisa, Lisa, Caity, Kerris and Brett: the team.

The color illustrations in this book were made with Plasticine that is shaped and pressed onto illustration board.
The drawings were done with ink and watercolor paint.

Photography by Ian Crysler.

Library of Congress Cataloging-in-Publication Data

Reid, Barbara, 1957-
Perfect snow / Barbara Reid.
p. cm.
Audience: Ages 5-8.
ISBN-13: 978-0-8075-6492-9
ISBN-10: 0-8075-6492-3
1. Snow—Juvenile fiction. 2. Snowmen—Juvenile fiction. 3. Boys—Juvenile fiction.
[1. Snow—Fiction. 2. Snowmen—Fiction. 3. Schools—Fiction.] I. Title.
PZ7.R2646Pe 2011
813.54—dc22
[[E]]
2010045643

Text and illustrations copyright ©2009 by Barbara Reid.
First published by North Winds Press, an imprint of Scholastic Canada.
Published in 2011 by Albert Whitman & Company.
10 9 8 7 6 5 4 3 2 1 BP 15 14 13 12 11

For more information about Albert Whitman & Company, visit our website at www.albertwhitman.com.

It came in the night.
"Perfect!" said Scott.

"SNOW!" said Jim.

Scott got ready in a hurry.

"Put on your corduroy pants!" his mother called. "And your woolly socks!"

Jim flew to the kitchen. "SNOW!"

A snow day would be perfect.

His sister yawned. "School is open, the radio said so."

"No problem," said Jim. "Recess will be great!"

Scott scanned the horizon.

"Snow!"

Jim packed a handful.

"Perfect!"

"Hurry up," Scott's mother called. "We'll be late!"

"Good morning, Jim," said Mrs. B. "I am sure you remember that throwing snow is not allowed."

Scott worked quietly at his desk.

Jim watched the clock. "At last! Conditions are perfect to build my totally massive, indestructible Snow Fortress of Doom."

The recess bell set off a stampede. Kids swarmed
the snow like ants on a dropped ice cream cone.

Jim claimed a spot and started construction.

Scott fought his way to the edge of the crowd.

"I will make the World's Greatest Snowman," said Scott. "This snow is perfect."

But the snowman was not so great.

"That was good practice," Scott decided. He made another.

"Could be better." He made a third.

"I know," he said. "I can make the world's greatest *team* of snowmen."

Building an indestructible fort was not so easy. More snow! Everybody wanted more snow.

Jim's fort was raided.

"That's my snow!"

"Finders keepers!"

The chase was on! Jim was caught up in a crazy twister of kids, whirling through the schoolyard, scooping up snow, scattering hats, and smashing everything in its path.

From the eye of the storm, Jim spotted Scott. The blizzard of destruction was heading straight for the little group of snowmen. They would be flattened for sure.

In a flash Jim jumped clear
of the mob and yelled,
"Here comes Mrs. B.!"

Everybody froze.

Just in time, the bell rang.

At lunchtime, Scott got back outside in a hurry.

"Nice snowmen," said Jim.

Scott nodded.

"I know a way you could make them stronger," said Jim.

Together they outlined a plan.

Everyone stopped to watch.

"Cute snowmen!"

"Cool fort!"

"Can we help?"

Scott nodded.

"More snow," said Jim.
"We need more snow!"

"There's fresh snow over here."

"We can use my old fort."

"Pack it harder!"

"Pile it higher!"

In no time an army of helpers was hauling snow
from every corner of the yard.

With wet mitts and frozen fingers they raced to
finish two more snowmen — the biggest of all.

Everyone held their breath as Scott carefully
set the last snowball into place.

"The World's Greatest Totally Massive Snowman Fort!" Jim announced.

Scott tossed his hat in the air. The crowd went wild.

It was all Mrs. B. could do to herd them back inside when the bell rang.

The whole school smelled like wet boots.

At the end of the day the boys watched
over the snowmen until the yard emptied.

"Perfect snow," said Jim.

Scott nodded.

It rained in the night.

"Slush!" said Jim.

"Excellent!" said Scott.

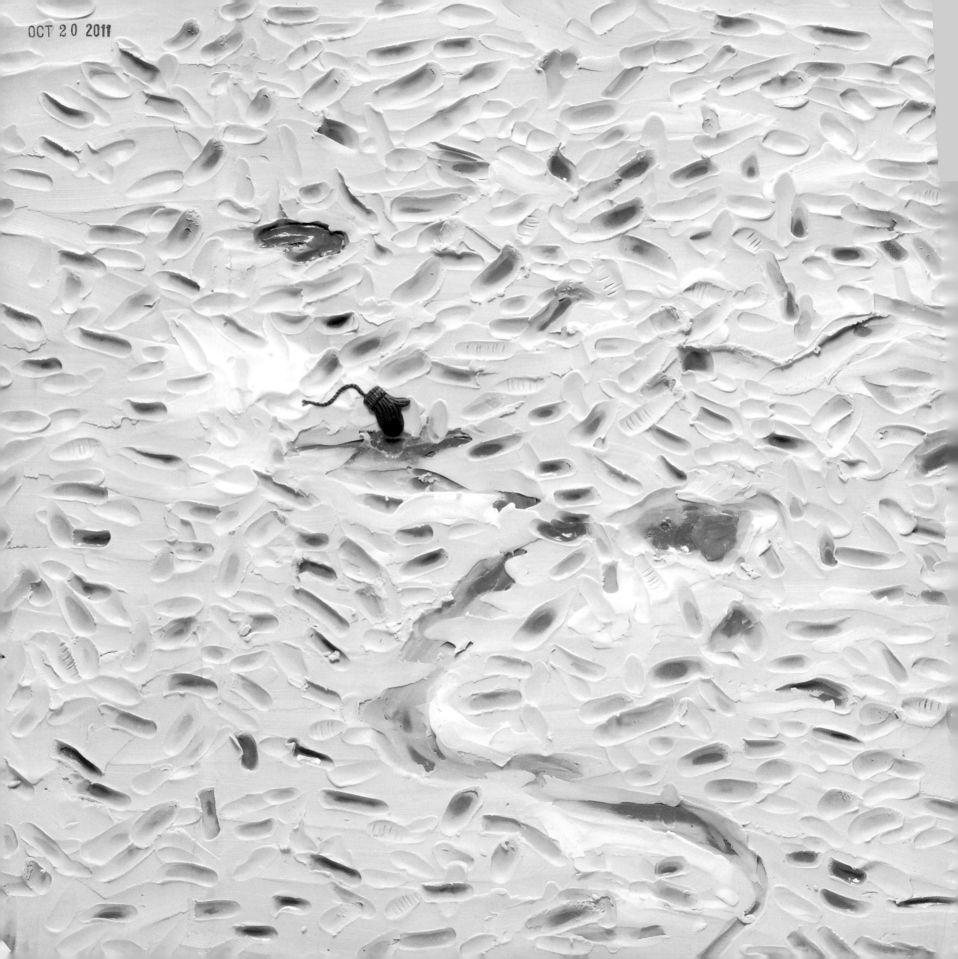
OCT 20 2011